P9-AOS-220

3 9082 14001 8543

FEB 0 9 2021

Trenton Veterans Memorial Library
2790 Westfield Rd.
Trenton, MI 48183
734-676-9777

JE KR

To Daisy and Jonah

Copyright © 2019 Clavis Publishing Inc., New York

Visit us on the Web at www.clavis-publishing.com.

No part of this publication may be reproduced or stored in a retrieval system,
or transmitted in any form or by any means, electronic, mechanical, photocopying,
recording, or otherwise, without the prior written permission of the publisher,
except in the case of brief quotations embodied in critical articles and reviews.
For information regarding permissions, write to Clavis Publishing, info-US@clavisbooks.com.

That's for Babies written by Jackie Azúa Kramer and illustrated by Lisa Brandenburg

ISBN 978-1-60537-455-0 (hardcover edition)
ISBN 978-1-60537-456-7 (softcover edition)

This book was printed in April 2019 at Nikara, M. R. Štefánika 858/25, 963 01 Krupina, Slovakia.

First Edition
10 9 8 7 6 5 4 3 2 1

Clavis Publishing supports the First Amendment and celebrates the right to read.

Jackie Azúa Kramer & Lisa Brandenburg

THAT'S FOR BABIES

Clavis

NEW YORK

The morning of Prunella's birthday,
the first thing she said was . . .
"I'm a BIG kid now."

She looked at her favorite doll, Talking Sally.
*"That's for **babies!**"*

And she packed her away in a box of old toys.
"Goodbye," chimed Sally.

"Good morning, Pru," said her mother.
"Heart-shaped pancakes for breakfast?"

*"That's for **babies!**"*

"*A-B-C-1-2-3,*" sang her father.
"Sing along, Pru."

"That's for babies!"

Animal cookies were too CUTESY.

The bubble had BURST on bubble baths.

Tuck-ins at bedtime were for TODDLERS.

"Hi, Pru," said her mother.
"Going somewhere?"

"*Now that I'm a BIG kid, it's time for adventure.*"

"Let's all go together," said her father.

At the park, other kids squealed
and screamed on the super swirly slide.
*"That's for **babies!**"*

At the library, other kids played pretend at story time.
*"That's for **babies**!"*

At the candy store, other kids licked double-scoop ice cream cones.
*"That's for **babies**."*

Even at a playdate, Prunella sat alone.
*"That's for **babies!**"*

Back at home, Prunella took Sally out of the dusty box.
"I've missed you. Being a big kid isn't fun."
"Let's have a tea party," chimed Sally.
"I'll get the animal cookies!"

"Sorry, Sally," sighed Prunella.
"No more tea parties.

I forgot . . .
*that's for **babies**.*"

That night, Prunella went to bed
as dark clouds filled her bedroom window.
"I'm not scared," whispered Prunella.
*"That's for **babies**."*

The wind whipped through the curtains.
"Well, maybe a little scared."

Flashes of lightning lit the dark sky
and zigzagged across the box of cast-off toys.

"Sally, are you scared in there?"
BOOOOM!
Thunder boomed through the house.

"Don't be scared! I'm here!"

"Good morning, Pru," said her parents.

"Sally got scared."

"That storm was loud and scary," they agreed.
"You're a brave girl."
"Even big kids get scared sometimes, Sally," said Prunella.

Prunella and Sally were ready for a busy day.
They made mud-licious mud pies.
"A small piece for you and a BIG piece for me!"

They launched to the moon
off the super swirly slide.

"Three—two—one . . . liftoff!"

They wore matching sparkly dresses
for afternoon tea.
"One lump or two?"

They flew on unicorns
to a faraway kingdom.

"Let's go visit a princess!"

They had a bubble bath and were tucked in to bed together.
"Pru, we know you're a big girl," said her parents.
"But if Sally or you are ever scared, you can always sleep in our bed."

"I know," said Prunella.
*"But that's for babies . . .
and **big kids** like me!"*

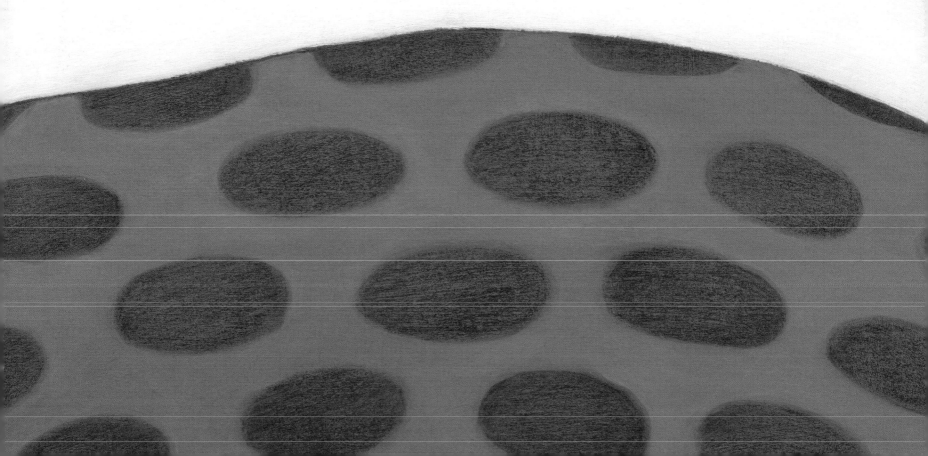